D1378579

For Margot,
who is truly creativealicious!
—V.K.

HarperFestival is an imprint of HarperCollins Publishers.

Pinkalicious: Purpledoodles
Copyright © 2012 by Victoria Kann, Inc.

PINKALICIOUS and all related logos and characters
are trademarks of Victoria Kann, Inc. Used with permission.

Based on the HarperCollins book *Purplicious* written by
Victoria Kann and Elizabeth Kann, illustrated by Victoria Kann

ISBN 978-0-06-208586-3

12 13 14 15 16  SCP  10 9 8 7 6 5 4 3 2 1
❖
First Edition

# Pinkalicious®
# Purpledoodles

## By Victoria Kann

Drawings by Carolina Farias
Based on the art of Victoria Kann
from the book *PURPLICIOUS*

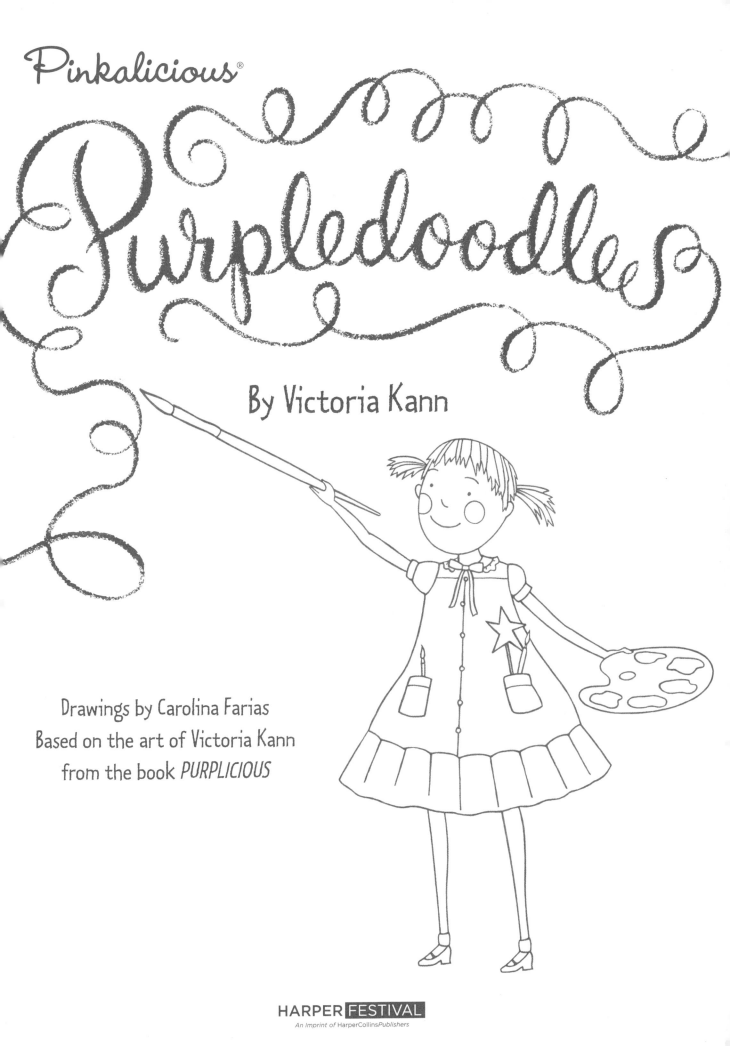

HARPER FESTIVAL
An Imprint of HarperCollinsPublishers

This book belongs to

_____ alicious.

Write your name here.

The only people allowed to draw in this book are

_____!

_____!

_____!

_____!

# Dear Purple Lovers,

Have you ever read the picture book *Purplicious?* In the story, Pinkalicious makes a new friend in art class who is painting a picture of a cake. She shows Pinkalicious the power of pink by mixing pink and blue paint together to make purple paint. Not only is purple pretty, it is purplicious!

Use this book to inspire your inner artist. Pick up your sparkly pens, paint, markers, crayons, and glue stick and fill this book with pinks, purples, and ALL the colors that make you feel happylicious. Create your own amazing modern art, give Pinkalicious an outfit worthy of a princess, and draw the most delicious ice-cream sundae in the world!

Make your drawings BIG, small, or teensy tiny.

Most of all, stay true to yourself

and have a PURPLICIOUS time!

*With pink love*
*and purple hugs,*
*Victoria*

# A Passion for Pink . . . and PURPLE!

Everybody knows that Pinkalicious loves the color pink. One day at school all the girls decide that pink stinks and black is the new "in" color. When Pinkalicious does not agree with the crowd, they tease her. She develops a bad case of the blues and wonders if anyone out there shares her love for all things pink. Pinkalicious learns how to stay true to herself and discovers that pink isn't just a pretty color. Pink is powerful because when it is mixed with blue it makes purple.

Purplicious forever!

# The Pinkerton Family Is Colorlicious

Color them in using all your favorite colors!

Mr. Pinkerton

Mrs. Pinkerton

Pinkalicious

Peter

What are the colors that Pinkalicious is going to use?
Add them to the palette.

What is Pinkalicious painting?
Draw it on the canvas.

JOKE: What color is a burp?

Answer: Burple!

You're in Pinkalicious's art class! Draw yourself painting the picture. What are you painting? Use your favorite colors.

There are ten paintbrushes hidden in this room!
Circle them. Then draw five more paintbrushes wherever you want!

Answer key on page 128.

# Did You Know?

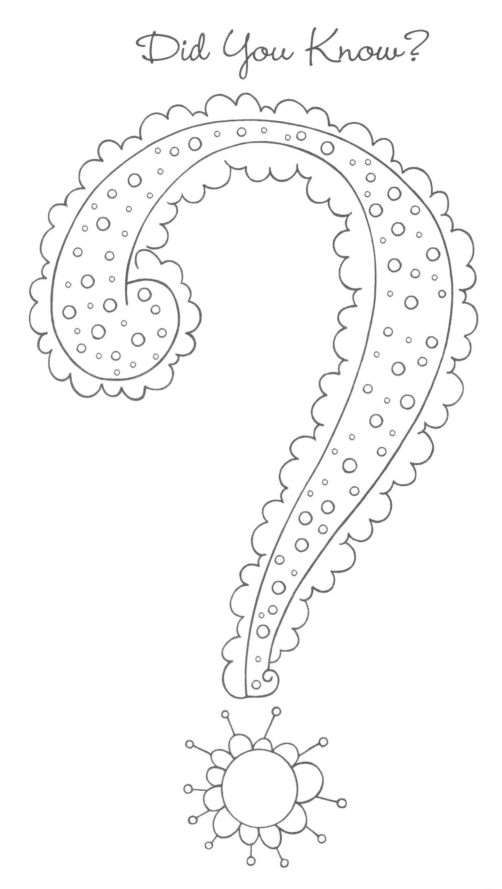

Purple is considered a royal color because many years ago princesses, princes, kings, queens, and the very wealthy were the only ones who could afford the rare and expensive purple dyes!

# Modern Art

Extend these squiggle lines to the edge of the canvas.

Don't get caught in the maze!

Enter

Exit

Can you fill in this canvas with circles, squares, and triangles?

What colors do you think look good together?
Color in the shapes and backgrounds
to make beautiful color combinations.

Representational pictures are pictures that look
just like what you would see in real life.
Draw a representational picture of your favorite animal.

An abstract picture is one that doesn't look exactly like something.
It's made of patterns and shapes and colors.
Draw the same animal, only this time make your picture abstract.

Can you finish Pinkalicious's painting of a sunset?
Don't forget to add the hills and clouds!

You have Pinkalicious's magic wand!
What wish would you make come true?
Draw it here!

Beatrice, Pauline, and Sophia love the color black.
Color in their outfits with the colors that YOU like!

# Passé is a French Word for Behind the Times

Draw a line and match the correct word to the passé object.

top hat

typewriter

record

bonnet

fountain pen

Model T car

A beret is a type of French hat often worn by artists.
Look at the beret above and then draw one for Pinkalicious to wear!

The pictures below are all called the same thing in French and English.
Color them in!

Palette

Croissant

Macramé

Escargot

Cul - de - sac

*Soirée*

*Silhouette*

*Chauffeur*

*Ballet*

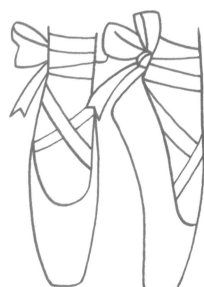

*Mousse*

# One Bird Isn't Like the Others

Circle the one that is different.

# Purpledoodle One-Minute Challenge

What can you make out of this shape in one minute? GO!

Pinkalicious and the girls need hula hoops!
How many hoops can they use at once? Draw them in.

The girls need new hairstyles!

# Boys Like the Color Pink, Too

Color in Peter, and don't forget to add some pink!

Pinkalicious stands up for what she believes in!
Draw the expressions of the kids on the bus when Pinkalicious
says to them, "You don't have to be a baby or a little girl to like the
color pink. Pink is for everyone. Even my brother likes pink."

Pinkalicious rides the bus to school. Draw yourself going to school!
Do you walk? Ride a bike? Fly in a helicopter?

# Has anyone ever teased you for the things you like?

Fill in the blanks with one of the choices below or make up your own answer.

I know a lot of people who like to
eat _____,
but I like to eat _____.

(olives, sardines, black licorice, green tea ice cream)

Some people like to play with _____,
but I like to play with _____.

(stuffed animals, dolls, toy cars, insects)

Many people think it is fashionable
to wear _____,
but I like to wear _____.

(flip-flops all day, a shirt that is too big for me, a funny hat)

Everyone seems to be listening to music
by _____ ,
but I like to sing LOUDLY to

_____ .

(opera, camp songs, show tunes)


Some people read books
about _____ ,
but I like to read

_____ .

(picture books, poems, the encyclopedia, mysteries, the phone book)

I am a unique person!

# Courage!

List three things that you would stand up for even if people teased you.

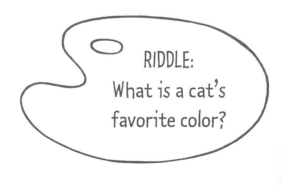

RIDDLE:
What is a cat's
favorite color?

Answer: Purr-ple!

Find the words in this word search listed in the key below.

```
S O T N C J P H C J A X
U N D E R W E A R A G D
I H Y T A Y A X A C D O
T F P X Y A R F B K H L
C A Y G O F L A B S F L
A X F H N A S X I T X H
S P I D E R F R T Q P O
E P A T R G L G F Y U U
H A F H Q L A M P L I S
G L A S S E S P R G Y E
X T H X T Y F H A P B Y
T O O T H B R U S H X T
R O L L E R S K A T E S
```

Answer key on page 128.

**KEY:** SUITCASE, SPIDER, UNDERWEAR, PEARLS, DOLLHOUSE, TOOTHBRUSH, GLASSES, ROLLERSKATES, CRAYON, JACKS, RABBIT, LAMP

# Pinkalicious Loves Pink

Finish drawing the objects in Pinkalicious's room. Then color them in.

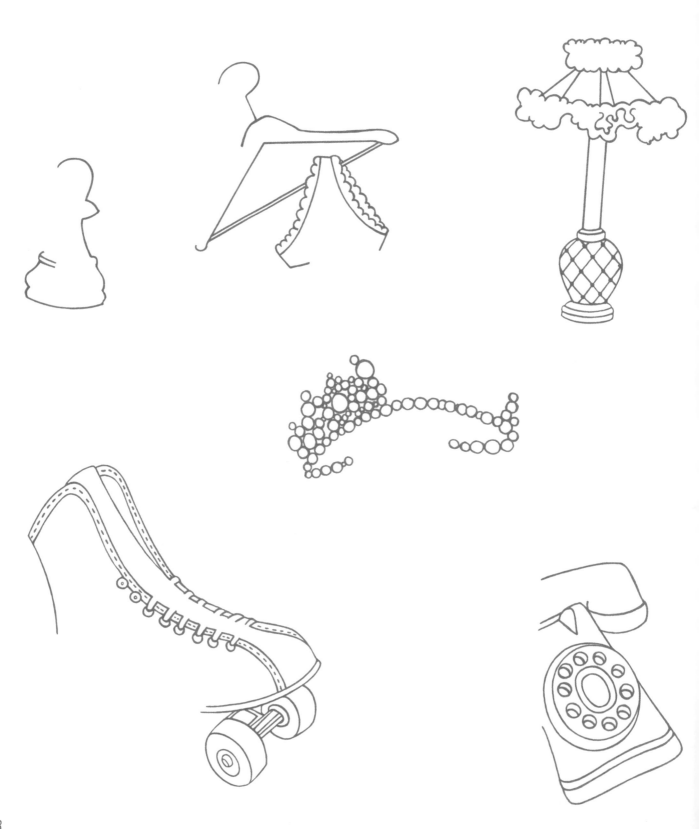

Draw your favorite thing in your room!

I love my....

Fill Pinkalicious's dollhouse with furniture!

What should Pinkalicious wear today?

# Purpledoodle!

Can you make a picture with these swirls?

The only black thing Pinkalicious owns
is a plastic spider left over from Halloween.
Draw a big, scary spider!

Here are some black things that you might have.
Color them in—using whatever colors you like!

Finish the book covers!

Paa Paa
Purple Sheep

Little Boy Purple

The Purple
Pony

Pinkocchio

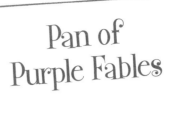

Pan of
Purple Fables

Pinkly Ever After

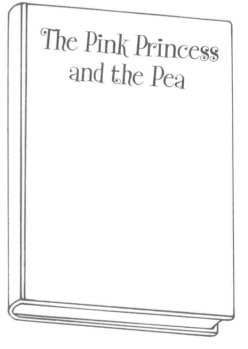

The Pink Princess
and the Pea

Finish drawing the flowers. Then add your own!

Draw someone riding Peter's hobby horse!

# Purpledoodle!

Can you make a picture with these squiggles?

# Peter Likes All Kinds of Hats

He likes baseball caps, cowboy hats, top hats, bowler hats, hard hats, and even propeller beanie hats. Give Peter a hat!

# Pink is perfect.
# Black is boring.

Finish the rest of the sentences.

Purple is p_____.

Blue is b_____.

Red is r_____.

Green is g_____.

Yellow is y_____.

A Purple Emperor butterfly has wings that shine purple in the light!
Finish drawing this butterfly.

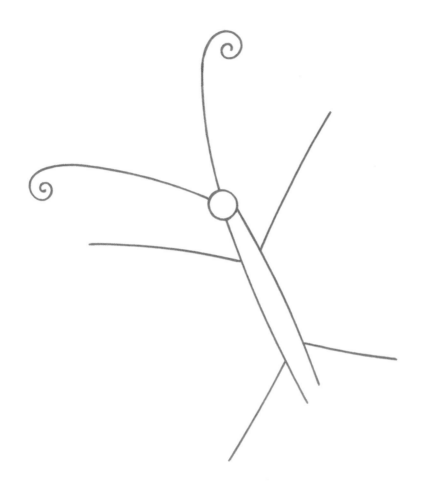

RIDDLE:
What is purple but
smells like green paint?

Answer: Purple paint!

What happened to you this week? Write about it in your diary.

Wednesday

Friday

Thursday

69

Finish the sentences below.

I am who I am and I like

_____.

(your favorite color)

_____ makes me happy

(your favorite color, place, or thing)

but _____

(something that makes you unhappy)

makes me sad.

_____ is a

(a color)

_____ color.

(a feeling)

_____ has no purpose.

(a color, place, or thing)

# Which bed is different?
## Color it in!

Answer key on page 128.

Who is riding the bike? Finish drawing the scene and color it in!

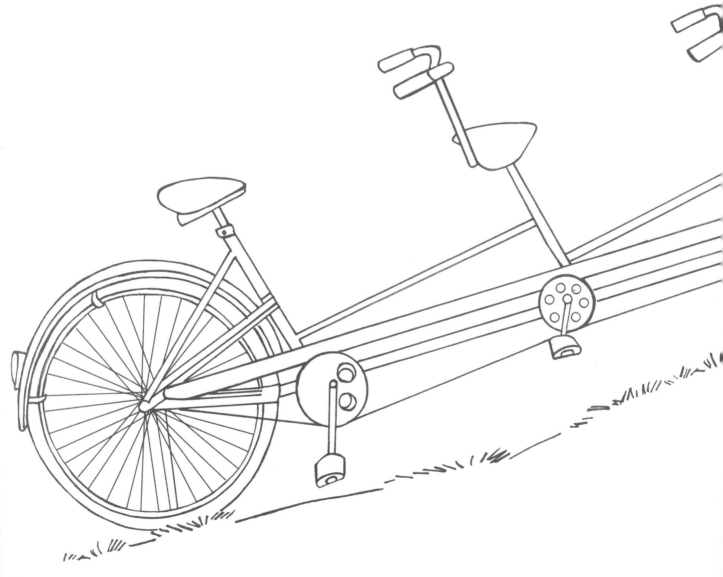

Pinkalicious wants some Magenta Mint Mango ice cream.
Help her get to the ice-cream shop!

START

Monday
Pink is still Perfect.

FINISH

Ice Cream

Mr. Swizzle's ice-cream shop looks just like an ice-cream cone!

Draw a bakery that looks like a cake!
Don't forget to add windows and a door!

Draw a library that looks like a book!

Draw a flower shop that looks like a flower!

Draw a school that looks like a pencil!

Mr. Swizzle's moustache, tie, and hat are missing!
Find them and draw them in.

Give everyone a curly mustache like Mr. Swizzle.

Now draw your family—and give them curly mustaches!
Don't forget your pets!

Finish the drawings.

Magenta
Mint Mango

Pink Passion
Fruit Paradise

Pleasing
Pomegranate
Punch

Vanilla

Plum Pink
Perfection

Draw the ice-cream sundae of your dreams, and name it!
Don't forget to add a cherry on top!

Sundae

# Can You Say This Three Times Fast?

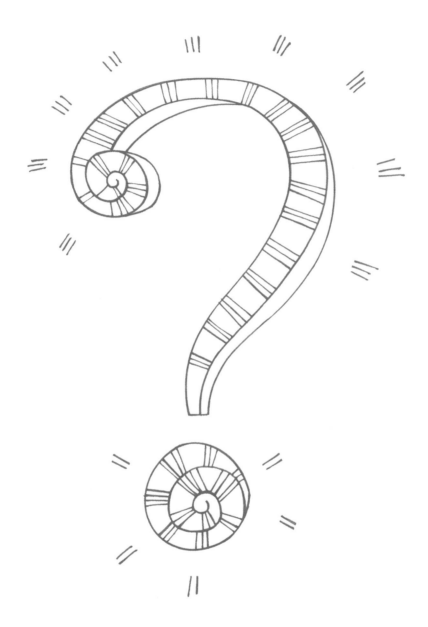

Pinkalicious, the pretty Princess of Pink, and Peter,
her princely brother, polished off a pound of pretzels,
then proceeded to play a pinkatastic game of pink-pong perfectly,
while prancing to a popular polka in purple pajamas!

The kids in school don't like the color pink.
This gives Pinkalicious the blues!

Draw Pinkalicious's face when she has the blues.

Now draw your own face when you have the blues.

**Did you know . . .**
Having the blues means
feeling sad, and seeing red
means being angry!

Why are Mr. and Mrs. Pinkerton and Peter surprised?
Add Pinkalicious and finish the picture.

# Purpledoodles
## One-Minute Challenge

What can you make out of this shape in one minute? GO!

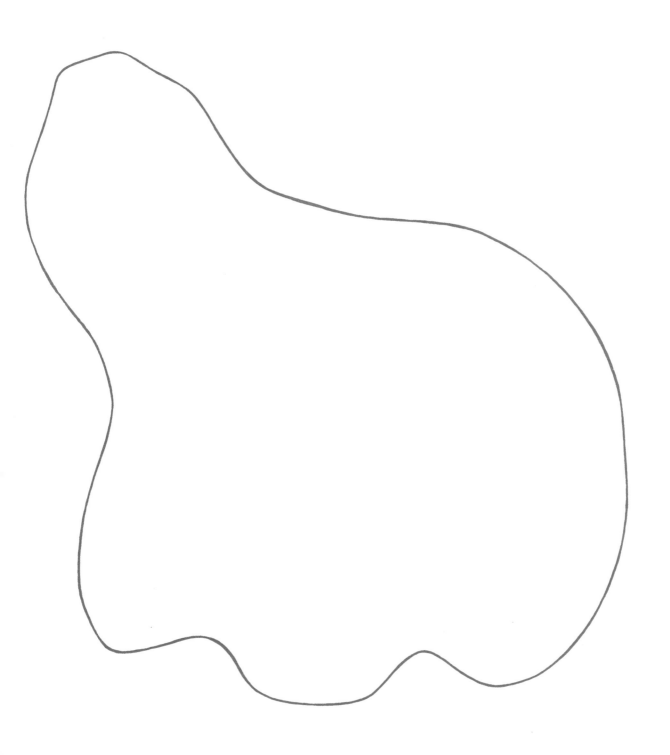

What is Pinkalicious thinking about?

The shining stars want to cheer up Pinkalicious.
Give the stars friendly faces.

The Pinkertons' house has all kinds of wallpaper.
Create your own wallpaper here!

When you feel alone, what do you do to feel better?
Finish the sentences.

Sometimes when I am going to sleep I feel alone,

so I _____

_____

_____

_____ ,

and then I feel better.

If I don't have anyone to play with I feel lonely,

but I _____

_____

_____

_____ ,

and it makes me feel happy.

If I wake up in the middle of the night and everyone is asleep, I _____

_____

_____

_____,

and then I can go back to sleep and have sweet dreams.

If the house is so quiet that I get worried, I

_____

_____

_____

_____,

and then I feel better.

When you mix colors, you get new colors! Color in the drawings.

**White + Red =**

hint: color of a

**Red + Yellow =**

hint: color of a

**Yellow + Blue =**

hint: color of

Answer key on page 128.

# Purple Is Powerful

Fill in the colors you need to mix to get purple!

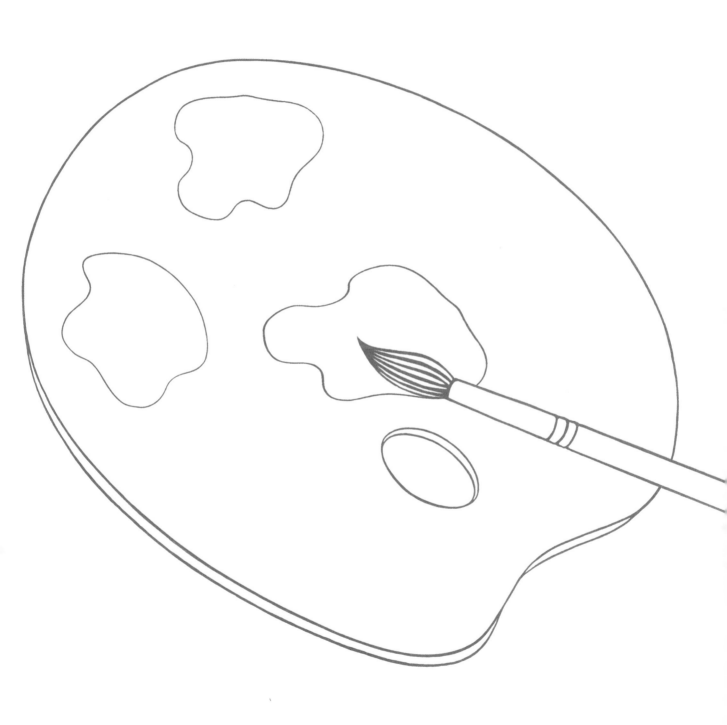

Circle the tools that you need to paint a painting.

# Did You Know ?

There are more than 1,000 shades of purple.
Here are just a few. Have you seen any of these colors?

| | |
|---|---|
| Lilac | Pansy purple |
| Lavender | Mulberry |
| Violet | Orchid |
| Royal purple | Electric purple |

# Purple Is Pretty

Make the cake look purplicious!

Give Pinkalicious a purplicious princess outfit!

Finish drawing Pinkalicious and her new friend, Lila.

# Everything Here Is Purple

Color the objects.

# STOP! DON'T TURN BACK!

Close your eyes and try to remember as many items as possible from the last two pages. Now draw them all here. And remember: no peeking!

Pinkalicious and Lila are getting
dressed up for an art show.
Design the perfect outfits
for them, and don't forget to
show how they're feeling!

What are Pinkalicious and Lila talking about?

Make a poem out of the word PURPLICIOUS.
Don't forget to read it out loud!

Here's a poem for the word PINK to help get you started!

Pinkalicious
Impressive
Nifty
Kind

P _____

U _____

R _____

P _____

L _____

I _____

C _____

I _____

O _____

U _____

S _____

# Purpledoodle!

Can you make a picture out of these loop-the-loops?

# Make this outfit purpletastic!

Create your own purplicious masterpiece!

# Do You Speak Purple?

Purple in Italian is **viola**

Purple in French is **pourpre**

Purple in German is **lila**

Purple in Spanish is morada

Purple in Japanese is 紫

Purple in Hindi is बैंगनी

Purple in Korean is 자주색

Purple in Danish is lilla

Purple in Chinese is 紫

# Use These Pages for
# Oodles of Purpledoodles

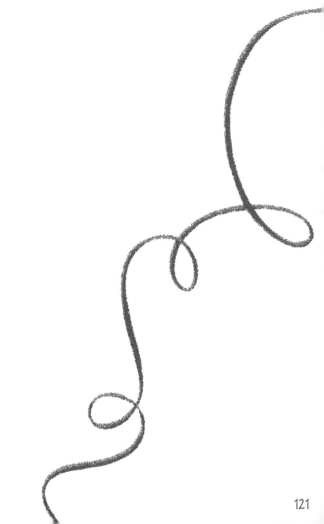

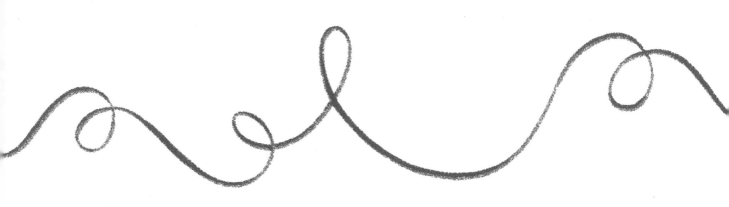

# Answer Key

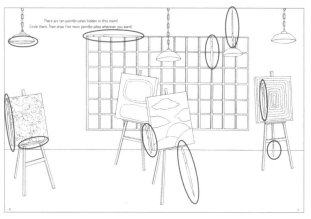

Pages 16–17

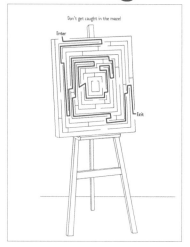

Page 20

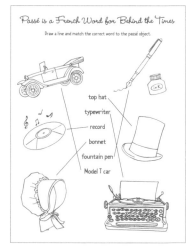

Page 30

Page 34

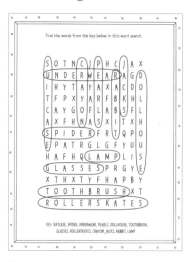

Page 47

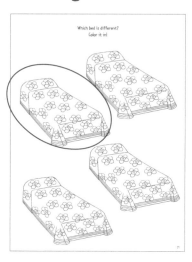

Page 71

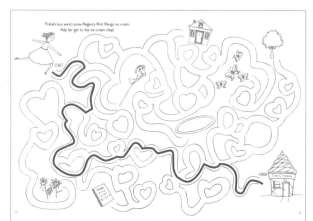

Pages 74–75

Page 100: White + red = pink; Red + yellow = orange;
Yellow + blue = green

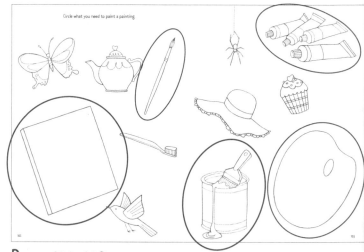

Page 102–103